STONE SOUP
with
MATZOH BALLS

A Passover Tale in Chelm

This
PJ BOOK
belongs to

_____

_____

PJ Library®

JEWISH BEDTIME STORIES and SONGS

Linda Glaser

Illustrated by
Maryam Tabatabaei

Albert Whitman & Company
Chicago, Illinois

To my mother, who has read to me all my life
and given me the incomparable joy of hearing
stories brought to life by a true master—L.G.

To my family for their love
and support—M.B.

Library of Congress Cataloging-in-Publication Data is on file with the publisher.

Text copyright © 2014 by Linda Glaser.
Illustrations copyright © 2014 by Albert Whitman & Company.
Published in 2014 by Albert Whitman & Company.
ISBN 978-0-8075-7620-5
Printed in China.
10 9 8 7 6 5 4 3 2 1 BP 18 17 16 15 14 13

The design is by Nick Tiemersma.

For more information about Albert Whitman & Company,
visit our web site at www.albertwhitman.com.

031415K1

Some people say that Chelm is a village of fools. That may or may not be true. You can decide for yourself. Listen to what happened one Passover when, right before sundown, a poor, ragged stranger arrived and changed the village forever.

"You know what we say at Passover," the stranger proclaimed to the people in the square. "All who are hungry come and eat." He looked around hopefully.

The people of Chelm all looked around too, hoping someone else would invite this hungry stranger in for the Seder.

"We hardly have enough food for ourselves," moaned Faigel.

"It's been such a long winter," groaned Lila.

"Do your belly a favor and go to the next town." Shmuel pointed the way.

Everyone nodded. But the stranger wouldn't budge.

"No food?" He shrugged. "Don't worry!" He pulled a stone from his pocket and held it up. "I can make the most delicious matzoh ball soup with this. All I need is a big cooking pot."

"Impossible!" exclaimed the people of Chelm.
"We're not fools. We know it takes more than a stone to make matzoh ball soup. Everyone knows you also need water!"

So Mendel and Yonkel ran and got the biggest pot, sloshing full of water.

Meanwhile the stranger made a fire. He placed the pot over the fire and dropped the stone in. Soon the water was boiling.

Yenta peered in. "*Humph!* I don't see any matzoh balls."

"You expect miracles in seconds?" asked the stranger. "First I need a ladle."

So Yenta hurried and got one.

The stranger dipped the ladle into the pot. He poured a little into his cup and took a sip. "*Ahh.*" He rubbed his belly. "For me— a poor stranger—this is delicious. But…" He looked around. "For the good people of Chelm, it could use a little salt."

"No problem." Golda raced home and brought back a saltshaker in no time.

The stranger sprinkled salt like there was no tomorrow.
He took another sip. "Now this is good enough for a king! But…"
He shook his head. "Not good enough for the people of Chelm.
You don't happen to have any onions in this town?"

"You think we're uncivilized? Of course we have onions!"
Moishe sent the children racing home.

They hurried back with enough onions
to make you cry for a week—maybe two.

Before you could blink, the stranger had a mountain of chopped onions. As he dumped them into the pot, he asked, "Here in Chelm, have you heard of garlic?"

"You think we're fools? Of course we've heard of garlic!"
Zaydel sent the children rushing home again. They hurried back
with enough garlic to choke a horse—maybe two.

The stranger hummed as he dropped the garlic into the pot.
"I suppose carrots are too common for you people of Chelm."

"Too common? *Bah!*" cried Yossel. "Feet are common too. But does that mean we don't use them? Don't be foolish. In Chelm we use our feet and our carrots."

And so it went…
carrots,
celery,
chicken…what a soup!

"*Humph!*" Yenta narrowed her eyes. "Don't think we don't know what you're doing." She shook her finger at the stranger. "What do you mean?" The stranger stopped stirring.

"You said you'd make matzoh ball soup from a stone." Yenta
stood on tiptoes so she could glare at him eyeball to eyeball.
"You think we're fools?" she cried.
"Of course not," said the stranger.

Yenta put her hands on her hips. "Then where are the matzoh balls?"

"What a wise woman!" said the stranger. "I almost forgot. That stone of mine makes the best matzoh balls in the world—so big and heavy they'll sit in your belly like rocks all eight days of Passover. Guaranteed. You won't need to eat for a week. I'll get them going right now!"

"Wait!" exclaimed Rifka. "Don't you know you're in Chelm?
Don't you know we make matzoh balls so light they can almost fly?"
   "Impossible!" said the stranger. "I've never met people like you.
So wise, so clever. And you can even make matzoh balls?"

"The very best!" The women all hurried home and soon dozens—no, hundreds—of matzoh balls were plopping into the pot.

The soup bubbled away and everyone in Chelm gawked. "Amazing," they exclaimed. "That's some stone."

The rabbi stroked his beard and nodded. "It's a miracle— right before our eyes."

The stranger tried another sip. "*Ahhh!* Now *this* is good enough for the people of Chelm."

It took four men to lug the pot into the synagogue—
the only place where everyone would fit for the Seder.

What a Seder! Plenty of wine and grape juice, piles of matzoh, and enough horseradish to make your toes curl for a year—maybe two.

When it was time for the meal, the stranger stood up.
He clanged the ladle against the soup pot.
"Good people of Chelm! I have something important to say."

A hush filled the room.

The stranger spread his arms wide and proclaimed,
"All who are hungry, please come and eat!"

Some say that the people of Chelm are all fools. But that Passover, everyone had a full belly—even the poor stranger. Now what's so foolish about that?

The Story of Passover

The first Passover happened long ago in the far-away country of Egypt. A mean and powerful king, named Pharaoh, ruled Egypt. Worried that the Jewish people would one day fight against him, Pharaoh decided that these people must become his slaves. As slaves, the Jewish people worked very hard. Every day, from morning until night, they hammered, dug, and carried heavy bricks. They built palaces and cities and worked without rest.

The Jewish people hated being slaves. They cried and asked God for help. God chose a man named Moses to lead the Jewish people. Moses went to Pharaoh and said, "God is not happy with the way you treat the Jewish people. He wants you to let the Jewish people leave Egypt and go into the desert where they will be free." But Pharaoh stamped his foot and shouted, "No, I will never let the Jewish people go!" Moses warned, "If you do not listen to God, many terrible things, called plagues, will come to your land." But Pharaoh would not listen, and so the plagues arrived. First, the water turned to blood. Next, frogs and, later, wild animals ran in and out of homes. Balls of hail fell from the sky and bugs, called locusts, ate all of the Egyptians' food.

Each time a new plague began, Pharaoh would cry, "Moses, I'll let the Jewish people go. Just stop this horrible plague!" Yet no sooner would God take away the plague than Pharaoh would shout, "No, I've changed my mind. The Jews must stay!" So God sent more plagues. Finally, as the tenth plague arrived, Pharaoh ordered the Jews to leave Egypt.

Fearful that Pharaoh might again change his mind, the Jewish people packed quickly. They had no time to prepare food and no time to allow their dough to rise into puffy bread. They had only enough time to make a flat, cracker-like bread called matzoh. They hastily tied the matzoh to their backs and ran from their homes.

The people had not travelled far before Pharaoh commanded his army to chase after them and bring them back to Egypt. The Jews dashed forward, but stopped when they reached a large sea. The sea was too big to swim across. Frightened that Pharaoh's men would soon reach them, the people prayed to God, and a miracle occurred. The sea opened up. Two walls of water stood in front of them and a dry, sandy path stretched between the walls. The Jews ran across. Just as they reached the other side, the walls of water fell and the path disappeared. The sea now separated the Jews from the land of Egypt. The Jews were free!

Each year at Passover, we eat special foods, sing songs, tell stories, and participate in a Seder—a special meal designed to help us remember this miraculous journey from slavery to freedom.